SIX SANDY SHEEP

For Larry Rosler and John O'Brien—
Thank you for our sheep . . .
We love ewes guys!
　　　　　　　—S. G. T. & J. R. E.

For Tess.
　　　—J. O'B.

Text copyright © 1997 by Judith Ross Enderle and Stephanie Gordon Tessler
Illustrations copyright © 1997 by John O'Brien

Published by Caroline House
Boyds Mills Press, Inc.
A Highlights Company
815 Church Street
Honesdale, Pennsylvania 18431
Printed in Mexico

Publisher Cataloging-in-Publication Data
Enderle, Judith Ross.
　　Six sandy sheep / by Judith Ross Enderle and Stephanie Gordon Tessler ; illustrated by John O'Brien.—1st ed.
[24]p. : col. ill. ; cm.
Summary : Six sheep can't seem to stay out of trouble when they go to the beach.
ISBN 1-56397-582-3
1. Sheep—Fiction—Juvenile literature. 2. Picture books—Juvenile literature. [1. Sheep—Fiction.] I. Tessler, Stephanie
Gordon. II. O'Brien, John, ill. III. Title.
　　　[E]—dc20　　　1997　　　AC　　　CIP
Library of Congress Catalog Card Number 96-83919

First edition, 1997
Book designed by Tim Gillner
The text of this book is set in 16-point Souvenir.
The illustrations are done in pen and ink with a combination of watercolors and dyes.

10 9 8 7 6 5 4 3 2

SIX SANDY SHEEP

by Judith Ross Enderle
and Stephanie Gordon Tessler

Illustrated by John O'Brien

Boyds Mills Press

Six sandy sheep spread out on the beach one sunny summer day.

SOON . . .

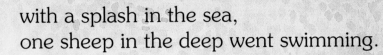

with a splash in the sea,
one sheep in the deep went swimming.

Now five sandy sheep showed off on the beach one sunny summer day.

SOON . . .

with a splash in the sea, one sheep in the deep went surfing.

Now four sandy sheep searched for shells
on the beach one sunny summer day.

SOON....

with a splash in the sea, one sheep in the deep went skiing.

Now three sandy sheep sipped sodas on the beach one sunny summer day.

SOON . . .

with a splash in the sea, one sheep in the deep went sailing.

Now two sandy sheep snapped shots on the beach
one sunny summer day.

SOON . . .

with a splash in the sea, one sheep in the deep went snorkeling.

Now one sandy sheep sifted sand on the beach
one sunny summer day.

SOON . . . .

with a splash in the sea, one sheep in the deep went skipping.

Now six dripping sheep came out of the sea one sunny summer day.
Then, in salty sea breezes, they stretched on the beach for snoozing.

UNTIL . . .

#28520069

E
END   Enderle, Judith
             Ross

             Six sandy sheep

DUE DATE	BRODART	04/98	14.95